A CHRISTMAS

CA

Evans

Published by Evans Brothers Limited
2A Portman Mansions
Chiltern Street
London W1U 6NR

© Evans Brothers Limited 2005
First published 2005

Printed in Hong Kong

British Library Cataloguing in Publication data
Francis, Pauline
        A Christmas carol. - (Fast track classics)
        1.Christmas stories 2.Children's stories
        I. Title. II. Dickens, Charles, 1812-1870. Christmas carol
        823.9'14 [J]

ISBN 0 237 52686 7

A CHRISTMAS CAROL

CHAPTER **One** *Humbug!*

CHAPTER **Two** *Marley's Ghost*

CHAPTER **Three** *A Warning*

CHAPTER **Four** *The First Ghost*

CHAPTER **Five** *The Second Ghost*

CHAPTER **Six** *Yes or No*

CHAPTER **Seven** *The Last Ghost*

CHAPTER **Eight** *The Dead Man*

CHAPTER **Nine** *To the Churchyard*

CHAPTER **Ten** *The End of It*

Introduction

Charles Dickens was born in 1812, the second of eight children. When he was twelve years old, his father went to prison because he owed money. Charles went out to work to help his family. He never forgot this terrible time when he was poor, and later used his experiences in some of his stories.

In his twenties, Charles found work writing about London life for newspapers and magazines. Some of these articles were published as a book called *Pickwick Papers*. This is how Charles Dickens became famous at the age of twenty-four.

A Christmas Carol, published in 1843, was the first of his Christmas stories. It tells the story of a ghost called Marley who comes to haunt his old friend Scrooge on Christmas Eve. He does this to teach him a lesson – not to be so mean. The word 'scrooge' is still used by some people today to describe a mean person.

Charles Dickens wrote many famous novels, including *Nicholas Nickleby*, *David Copperfield*, *Oliver Twist* and *Great Expectations*. He died in 1870 at the age of fifty-eight and is buried in Westminster Abbey, London.

CHAPTER ONE

Humbug!

Marley was dead – to begin with. And when Marley died, Ebenezer Scrooge was the only friend at his funeral.

Scrooge was a mean man – a greedy, tight-fisted man. He was as hard and as sharp as flint and secretive and solitary. The cold inside him froze his old face, nipped his pointed nose and shrivelled his cheeks. It made his eyes red and his thin lips blue. Frost seemed to shine on his head and his eyebrows. He was as bitter as the coldest wind.

Nobody ever stopped Scrooge in the street to say a friendly word. No beggar ever begged from him. No child ever asked him what time it was. Did Scrooge care? No! He liked more than anything else to keep people at a distance. And at Christmas he did not thaw out, not even by one degree.

Once upon a time, on Christmas Eve, old Scrooge was busy counting money. It was cold, bleak, foggy weather. It was only just after three o'clock in the afternoon but it was dark already. The door of Scrooge's office was open so that he could keep an eye on his clerk, Bob Cratchit. He was in a cold dark room copying letters by hand. His fire was so small that it looked like a single coal, but he could not make

it larger because Scrooge kept the coal in his room. The clerk tried to warm himself in front of his candle.

"A Merry Christmas, uncle!" a cheerful voice cried. It was the voice of Scrooge's nephew, Fred.

"Bah!" Scrooge replied. "Humbug!"

His nephew was so hot from walking in the fog and frost that his face glowed red and his eyes sparkled.

"I'm sure you don't mean that, uncle!" he replied.

"I do," Scrooge replied. "Merry Christmas, indeed! What right do *you* have to be merry? You're poor. Bah! Humbug!"

"Don't be cross, uncle!"

"What else do you expect me to be," Scrooge said, "when I live in a world full of fools? Merry Christmas! Christmas is just a time for paying bills when you haven't got enough money. If I had my way, every idiot who says "Merry Christmas" would be boiled in his own pudding. You celebrate Christmas in your own way and let me celebrate it in mine."

"But you don't celebrate Christmas!" his nephew replied. "It is a good time. It is the only time in a long year when men and women think of other people."

Bob Cratchit clapped loudly. Then he poked his fire again, putting out the last little spark.

"If I hear another sound from *you*," Scrooge shouted, "you will lose your job."

"Come and eat Christmas dinner with us tomorrow," his nephew begged.

"No," Scrooge replied. "Good afternoon to you."

"A Merry Christmas, uncle," his nephew said kindly. "And also to you, Bob Cratchit."

As he went out, two plump gentlemen came in. "Have I the pleasure of speaking to Mr Scrooge or Mr Marley?" one of them asked. "Both names are written on the door."

"Mr Marley has been dead for seven years," Scrooge told him. "He died seven years ago tonight."

"At this festive time of the year, Mr Scrooge," the gentleman continued, "we must all think of the poor who suffer greatly."

"Are there no prisons or workhouses for them?" Scrooge asked.

"There are," the gentleman replied. "But they hardly give cheer to the mind or body. That is why a few of us are starting a fund to buy meat and drink and something to keep the poor warm this Christmas. How much can you give, Mr Scrooge?"

"Nothing!" Scrooge replied. "I wish to be left alone. I do not make merry at Christmas. I help to support the prisons and the workhouses and those who are badly off must go there."

"Many would rather die than do that," the man replied.

"Then they must die," Scrooge said. "There are already too many people on this earth. Good afternoon, gentlemen!"

As soon as they had left, Scrooge went back to his work. Meanwhile, the fog and the darkness thickened and the cold grew worse. At last it was time to close the office.

"You'll want tomorrow off, I suppose?" Scrooge asked Bob Cratchit.

"If that is convenient, sir," his clerk replied.

"It's not convenient," Scrooge replied, "and it's not fair. Why should I pay you a day's wages for no work?"

"Christmas is only once a year, sir."

"A poor excuse!" Scrooge said. "But I suppose you must have the whole day. But you must start earlier the day after."

Scrooge left and ate alone at his usual inn. Then he went home to bed. He lived in rooms which had once belonged to Marley. They were very gloomy, hidden away in a house where nobody lived except Scrooge. All the other rooms were let as offices.

It was so dark that even Scrooge had to grope his way to his front door. And as he put his key in the lock, he stared in amazement. The shape of the doorknocker had changed – into Marley's face.

CHAPTER TWO

Marley's Ghost

The face was not angry. It looked at Scrooge as it used to look seven years ago, its ghostly spectacles sitting on its ghostly forehead. Its eyes were wide open, but they did not move. Its hair stood on end.

Scrooge stared at it. Then it became a doorknocker again. Scrooge was surprised, but he turned his key, walked inside and lit his candle. He looked carefully behind him as if he expected to see Marley's hair sticking out in the hall. There was nothing there.

Scrooge walked slowly up the stairs with his candle. But before he shut his heavy door, he walked through his rooms to make sure that everything was all right. There was nobody under the table, nobody under the sofa and nobody under the bed. Satisfied, he closed his door and locked himself in. Then he put on his dressing gown and slippers and sat down before the fire. It was a very small fire for such a cold night and he was forced to sit very close to it. And in the tiles around it, he saw Marley's face again.

"Humbug!" Scrooge said, getting up to walk around his room. Then he sat down again. As he put his head back in his chair, he glanced at a bell that hung in the room, one that had been used to call the servants. To his great astonishment, it began to swing. At first, it swung so softly that it hardly made a sound. But soon it rang out loudly. And so did every bell in the house.

The sound lasted for about a minute, but it felt like an hour. Suddenly, the bells stopped ringing. Another sound filled the air – a clanking noise deep down below as if somebody was dragging a heavy chain.

"They say that is the noise ghosts make in haunted houses!" Scrooge whispered to himself.

The noise grew louder. He heard it on the floor below his. Then it came up the stairs and straight towards his door.

"It's humbug!" Scrooge said. "I don't believe it."

Scrooge's face turned pale as the sound came through the heavy door and into his room. It was Marley. And he pulled a long chain made of cash-boxes, keys, padlocks and heavy purses.

Scrooge looked at his old partner. He looked straight through his waistcoat at the two buttons on the back of his coat. He did not believe his eyes, although the ghost was standing in front of him. And its paleness chilled him to the bone.

CHAPTER THREE

A Warning

"What do you want with me?" Scrooge asked, his voice as cold as ever. "Who are you?"

"Ask me who I *was*," the ghost replied.

"Who were you, then?" Scrooge asked, raising his voice.

"When I was alive, I was your partner, Jacob Marley. You don't believe in me," he said. "Yet you can see me with your own eyes."

"No, I don't," Scrooge told him. He was terrified, staring at those fixed eyes. "Humbug!" he said at last. "Humbug, I tell you!"

At these words, the ghost gave a terrible shout and shook its chain with a dreadful noise. Scrooge had to hold onto his chair tightly to stop himself from fainting. His horror was even greater when the ghost unwound the bandage around his head and let his jaw fall open wide. Scrooge fell onto his knees and put his hands over his face.

"Have mercy on me!" he cried. "Why have you come to haunt me like this?"

"Do you believe in me or not?" the ghost asked.

"I do," Scrooge replied. "But why have you come to *me*? Why are you wearing this chain?"

"I wear the chain I formed during my life," the ghost replied. "I made it, link by link, by the mean way in which I lived. You also are making such a chain, Scrooge, and it is a *very* heavy one."

Scrooge glanced at the floor but he could see nothing. Then he put his hands into his pockets as he usually did when he was thinking.

"I should have been kinder to my fellow-men," Marley's ghost said. "I suffer most at this time of the year. Listen to me, Scrooge. I am here to warn you so that you can escape my fate."

"You were always a good friend to me," Scrooge said, "and I thank you."

"You will be haunted by Three Ghosts," the ghost began.

Scrooge's face fell almost as low as Marley's.

"Without their visits," Marley continued, "you will not avoid the path that I have to walk along now. Expect the first Ghost tomorrow morning, when the clock strikes one."

"Couldn't they all come together so that it is over and done with?" Scrooge asked.

"Expect the second ghost the next night at the same time," he said. "The third will come the next night on the last stroke of twelve. Do not look for me again. And for your own sake, remember what has happened between us tonight."

As he spoke, Marley picked up the bandage from the table

and wrapped it around his jaw. Then he wound the chain round and round his arm. He began to move backwards towards the window, which raised itself slowly so that it was wide open when he reached it.

Marley's ghost beckoned Scrooge to follow him. As Scrooge reached the window, he heard strange noises in the air outside, wailing and shrieking. Marley joined in this mournful crying. Then he floated out into the dark night. Scrooge looked through the window. The air was filled with ghosts, restless and moaning. Every one of them wore chains like Marley's. To his surprise, Scrooge recognised some of them. Slowly these ghosts faded away and the night became dark and silent again. Scrooge closed the window. Then he went over to the door through which Marley's ghost had entered and examined it. It was still locked and bolted.

He tried to say, "Humbug!" but he could not.

CHAPTER FOUR

The First Ghost

When Scrooge woke up, it was so dark that he could hardly make out the difference between the walls and the window. A church clock began to strike. Scrooge jumped out of bed and groped his way to the window. He rubbed the frost from the glass with his sleeve, but he could see very little. It was still very foggy and cold. He went back to bed and lay there thinking.

"Marley's ghost must have been a dream," he decided.

But when the clock struck a quarter to one, Scrooge remembered what his friend had said.

"Marley told me to expect a ghost at one o'clock," he thought to himself. "I shall stay awake until then."

But Scrooge fell asleep and only woke up when the clock struck one. As the chime died away, a light flashed into the room and a hand pulled back the curtains around his bed. He came face to face with a strange figure – like a child, like an old man, it was difficult to tell. Its long hair was white, although its face had no wrinkles on it. Its arms and hands were long and muscular. Its skin was pink. Its delicate legs and feet were bare and it wore a tunic of the purest white trimmed with summer flowers. It held a branch of fresh holly

old Fezziwig!" Scrooge cried in amazemen

wig put down his pen and looked up at

seven o'clock in the evening.

!" he called. "Dick! Come in here! No m

. It's Christmas Eve!"

aw himself as a young man enter the roo

his friend Dick. Then in came a fiddler with

ved by Mrs Fezziwig and three Miss Fezziwi

came all the young men employed in

ey ate and danced until the clock struck elev

d Mrs Fezziwig stood by the door and sh

each person and wished them each "Me

When everybody had gone, the two apprenti

beds under a counter in the back-shop.

piness Mr Fezziwig gives only cost a f

it is as great as if he had spent a fortun

. He paused as the Ghost looked at him. "I w

inder to Bob Cratchit."

ke, Scrooge saw himself again. He was ol

face did not yet have the lines and harsh lo

ow. But it had begun to look tired and mean.

e. He was sitting next to a young girl dressed

eyes glinted with tears.

e changed, Ebenezer," she said. "We agreed

we were both young and poor – and happy to

ll free you from your promise. I know that y

and a hat.

But the strangest thing was the bright light around its head.

The figure changed shape all the time. Sometimes it was a shape with one arm, then one leg, now with twenty legs, now a pair of legs without a head, now a head without a body. Then suddenly, its shape came back again, as clear as ever.

"Are you the ghost, sir?" Scrooge asked.

"I am!" The voice was soft and gentle.

"Who and what are you?" Scrooge asked.

"I am the Ghost of Christmas Past," it replied. "*Your* past. And I am here to save you."

The Ghost put out a strong arm as it spoke and clasped Scrooge gently by the arm. "Walk with me!"

Scrooge wanted to go back to his warm bed, but the hand that held him was strong. It pulled him over to the window.

"I am a human being," Scrooge complained. "I shall fall."

The Ghost placed his hand upon Scrooge's heart. "Allow me to touch you there, and you will be held up," he said.

As he spoke, they passed through the wall and into the open countryside. The city of London had vanished, and the mist and darkness with it. It was a clear cold winter day with snow upon the ground. Scrooge looked about him.

"Good heavens!" he said. "I was born here."

They walked along the road. Scrooge knew the name of

every person they saw. Why was he so pleased to see them? Why did his eyes fill with tears? Why was he so happy when he heard them wish each other Merry Christmas? They came close to an old schoolhouse with broken windows and rooms that were cold and bare. A lonely boy sat reading at a desk, by a small fire.

"That child has been left alone at school," the Ghost said.

"I know," Scrooge replied, sobbing. *"I* was that boy! I wish… but it's too late now. There was a boy singing a Christmas carol at my door last night. I could have given him some money. But I didn't."

The Ghost smiled thoughtfully and waved his hand. "Let's see another Christmas!" he said.

The young Scrooge grew taller and he was walking up and down in the schoolroom, looking towards the door. It opened and a little girl ran in and kissed him.

"I have come to bring you home, dear brother!" she said, clapping her hands. "Home forever! And we'll all be together this Christmas and have a merry time."

Now they left the countryside where Scrooge grew up and came to a busy city. It was Christmas-time again. The Ghost stopped outside the door of a warehouse.

"Do you know this place?" it asked.

"Know it?" Scrooge replied. "I was an apprentice here."

They went inside. An old gentleman wearing a wig sat at a high desk, his head almost touching the ceiling.

and a hat.

But the strangest thing was the bright light around its head.

The figure changed shape all the time. Sometimes it was a shape with one arm, then one leg, now with twenty legs, now a pair of legs without a head, now a head without a body. Then suddenly, its shape came back again, as clear as ever.

"Are you the ghost, sir?" Scrooge asked.

"I am!" The voice was soft and gentle.

"Who and what are you?" Scrooge asked.

"I am the Ghost of Christmas Past," it replied. "*Your* past. And I am here to save you."

The Ghost put out a strong arm as it spoke and clasped Scrooge gently by the arm. "Walk with me!"

Scrooge wanted to go back to his warm bed, but the hand that held him was strong. It pulled him over to the window.

"I am a human being," Scrooge complained. "I shall fall."

The Ghost placed his hand upon Scrooge's heart. "Allow me to touch you there, and you will be held up," he said.

As he spoke, they passed through the wall and into the open countryside. The city of London had vanished, and the mist and darkness with it. It was a clear cold winter day with snow upon the ground. Scrooge looked about him.

"Good heavens!" he said. "I was born here."

They walked along the road. Scrooge knew the name of

every person they saw. Why was he so pleased to see them? Why did his eyes fill with tears? Why was he so happy when he heard them wish each other Merry Christmas? They came close to an old schoolhouse with broken windows and rooms that were cold and bare. A lonely boy sat reading at a desk, by a small fire.

"That child has been left alone at school," the Ghost said.

"I know," Scrooge replied, sobbing. "*I* was that boy! I wish… but it's too late now. There was a boy singing a Christmas carol at my door last night. I could have given him some money. But I didn't."

The Ghost smiled thoughtfully and waved his hand. "Let's see another Christmas!" he said.

The young Scrooge grew taller and he was walking up and down in the schoolroom, looking towards the door. It opened and a little girl ran in and kissed him.

"I have come to bring you home, dear brother!" she said, clapping her hands. "Home forever! And we'll all be together this Christmas and have a merry time."

Now they left the countryside where Scrooge grew up and came to a busy city. It was Christmas-time again. The Ghost stopped outside the door of a warehouse.

"Do you know this place?" it asked.

"Know it?" Scrooge replied. "I was an apprentice here."

They went inside. An old gentleman wearing a wig sat at a high desk, his head almost touching the ceiling.

"Why, it's old Fezziwig!" Scrooge cried in amazement.

Old Fezziwig put down his pen and looked up at the clock. It was seven o'clock in the evening.

"Ebenezer!" he called. "Dick! Come in here! No more work tonight. It's Christmas Eve!"

Scrooge saw himself as a young man enter the room, followed by his friend Dick. Then in came a fiddler with his music, followed by Mrs Fezziwig and three Miss Fezziwigs, smiling. In came all the young men employed in the business. They ate and danced until the clock struck eleven. Then Mr and Mrs Fezziwig stood by the door and shook hands with each person and wished them each "Merry Christmas". When everybody had gone, the two apprentices went to their beds under a counter in the back-shop.

"The happiness Mr Fezziwig gives only cost a few pounds, but it is as great as if he had spent a fortune," Scrooge said. He paused as the Ghost looked at him. "I wish I had been kinder to Bob Cratchit."

As he spoke, Scrooge saw himself again. He was older now, but he face did not yet have the lines and harsh look that he had now. But it had begun to look tired and mean. He was not alone. He was sitting next to a young girl dressed in black, whose eyes glinted with tears.

"You have changed, Ebenezer," she said. "We agreed to marry when we were both young and poor – and happy to be so. But I shall free you from your promise. I know that you no longer wish to marry a poor girl. May you be happy in the life you have chosen."

"Show me no more!" Scrooge shouted. "Take me home! Why do you torture me in this way?"

"One shadow more," the Ghost replied. He pinned Scrooge with his arms and forced him to watch. They were in a warm and comfortable room. Near to the winter fire sat the same girl, now a middle aged woman, surrounded by children. The door opened and their father came in, carrying Christmas toys and presents.

"I saw an old friend of yours this afternoon, dear," he told his wife. "Guess who it was?"

"Mr Scrooge," she said at last, laughing.

"It was!" her husband replied. "His partner Marley is dying, I hear. There he sat in the candlelight in his office. Quite alone in the world."

"Ghost of Christmas Past!" Scrooge said. "Take me away from this place."

"These are the shadows of your past life," the Ghost replied. "Do not blame *me* if you do not like them."

CHAPTER FIVE

The Second Ghost

Scrooge felt the Ghost fade away and he was soon in his bedroom again. He fell into a deep sleep and only woke up when the clock struck one o'clock.

"I must have slept through a whole day!" he said to himself. "But I have woken up just in time. Jacob Marley's messenger will be here soon. I shall draw back the curtains from my bed so that I can see it. I do not want to be taken by surprise again."

However, when the clock struck one no shape appeared, although a stream of light flooded into his room. Scrooge began to tremble violently. A quarter of an hour passed by, but the ghost did not come.

"I do not know what this means!" he cried to himself. "Perhaps the light is coming from the next room. I shall get out of bed and look."

Scrooge shuffled in his slippers towards the door. As soon as his hand was on the handle, a strange voice called out, "Come in, Scrooge!" Scrooge peeped around the door. It was his own room, there was no doubt about that. But it had changed. The walls and ceilings were covered with holly, mistletoe and ivy. An enormous fire blazed and roared up the

chimney.

Piled high on the floor of the room were turkeys, geese, chickens, mince pies, Christmas puddings, red-hot chestnuts, fruits and bowls of hot wine. On top of this pile sat the Ghost. It held up a glowing torch to Scrooge's face.

"Come in, Scrooge!" it cried again in a friendly voice,

"and get to know me better. I am the Ghost of Christmas Present. Look at me!"

Scrooge looked up. The Ghost wore a simple green robe edged with white fur. Its feet were bare and it wore on its head a holly wreath sparkling with shining icicles. Its dark brown curls hung loose.

"Take me where you wish," Scrooge said. "I was forced to travel last night and I learned a hard lesson, which I still remember. If you have anything to teach me, then teach me."

"Touch my robe!" the Ghost ordered.

Scrooge held onto it tightly. The room vanished at once and they were standing in the streets of London on Christmas morning. Snow lay everywhere. The sky was gloomy. But there was a feeling of cheerfulness everywhere as people shovelled the snow from their doorways and children threw snowballs.

The Ghost took Scrooge straight to Bob Cratchit's house. Bob was walking home from church carrying his son on his shoulder. Poor Tiny Tim could not walk without a crutch and iron rods on his legs. As soon as they reached the house, everybody got ready to eat their Christmas dinner.

Mrs Cratchit paused and looked at the carving knife in her hand. Then she plunged it into the goose and a gasp of delight ran along the table. Even Tiny Tim beat on the table with the handle of his knife and cried weakly, "Hurrah!"

"I have never eaten such a finely cooked goose," Bob Cratchit declared when his plate was empty.

Mrs Cratchit brought in the Christmas pudding, her face flushed and smiling proudly. In her hands, the pudding blazed with lighted brandy and was bright with holly.

"It's a wonderful pudding!" Bob Cratchit cried. "The best one yet!"

After they had eaten, the Cratchit family gathered around the fire where chestnuts spluttered noisily.

"A Merry Christmas to you all, my dears," their father said. "God bless us all."

"God bless us every one," Tiny Tim said.

Scrooge stared at the scene in front of him. "Tell me if Tiny Tim lives or not," he begged.

"If something is not done in the future, he will die," the Ghost replied.

"No, no!" Scrooge said. "Oh no, kind Spirit! Tell me that he will live."

"Let him die," the Ghost replied. "There are already too many people on this earth."

Scrooge hung his head in shame at the sound of his own words.

CHAPTER SIX

Yes or No

Scrooge and the Ghost left the Cratchit family and travelled on across a bleak moor towards the sea. And in every place – cottage, lighthouse, ship – every man had a kind word for his fellow men.

"I am surprised," Scrooge thought to himself, "to hear such merry laughter in such dark and lonely places."

As he listened, he recognised the sound of his own nephew's laughter. He saw that he was in a bright and gleaming room. Scrooge's nephew held his sides as he laughed. He made his wife laugh, too, and all their friends.

"Do you know what Scrooge said?" his nephew was saying, "that Christmas was a humbug!"

"Shame on him, Fred!" his wife said.

"He's a funny old fellow," Fred replied, "and not as pleasant as he could be. He will get what he deserves. But I have nothing to say against him."

"He is very rich," his wife said.

"His money is no use to him," her husband said. "I am sorry for him and I couldn't be angry with him if I tried. He is the only one who suffers. He will not have any pleasant memories by refusing to eat with us today. I do pity him."

After tea they had some music, for they were a musical family. Scrooge softened as he listened, recognising one of the tunes which his poor dead sister used to sing.

Then they played games. There were at least twenty people in that room, young and old; but they all played. And so did Scrooge.

"Please let me stay until the end of the party!" he begged the Ghost. "They are starting a new game. Give me just half an hour."

It was a game called "Yes" and "No". Scrooge's nephew had to think of something and his guests had to find out what it was. He could only answer "Yes" and "No" to their questions.

"An animal?" they asked, "a rather bad-tempered animal, one that growls and grunts and walks about the streets of London, but it doesn't live in a zoo?"

At every fresh question, the nephew burst into a fresh roar of laughter. At last, Fred's wife called out, "I know what it is! It's your Uncle Scrooge!"

"He has given us a great deal of amusement today," Fred said, "and so it would be ungrateful not to drink his health. Hold up your glasses and drink a toast to Uncle Scrooge."

"Uncle Scrooge!" everybody shouted.

"Are the lives of Ghosts short?" Scrooge asked as they travelled on. "I notice that you are growing older by the minute. Your hair is quite grey now."

"Yes," the Ghost replied. "My life on earth is *very* short. It ends tonight, at midnight. Listen, the time is near."

A clock was chiming a quarter to midnight.

As the Ghost spoke, Scrooge noticed a clawed foot sticking out from under the green robe. He brought out two children who knelt at his feet and clung to him. Their hands were shrivelled like those of an old person, their skin was yellow and their clothes were ragged. Scrooge stood back in surprise. He tried to speak but the words stuck in his throat.

"Are they yours?" he asked at last.

"No, they belong on earth," the Ghost said. "This boy is Ignorance. This girl is Poverty. They are both doomed to die."

"Is there no one who can help them?" Scrooge asked.

"Are there no prisons?" the Ghost asked, staring at Scrooge as he repeated Scrooge's own words. "Are there no workhouses?"

The clock struck twelve. As Scrooge looked at the Ghost, it disappeared. *"The third Ghost will come on the last stroke of twelve",* Scrooge muttered. "That's what Marley said."

As the last stroke stopped vibrating, Scrooge looked up and saw another ghost, draped and hooded. And it was coming along the ground like mist towards him.

CHAPTER SEVEN

The Last Ghost

When the Ghost had reached him, Scrooge knelt down and looked up at him. It was covered in black clothing. Only one hand could be seen. It did not speak or move and the sight of it filled Scrooge with dread.

"Are you the Ghost of Christmas Yet to Come?" Scrooge asked.

The Ghost did not answer, but pointed into the distance.

"You are going to show me the shadows of the things that have not happened yet?" Scrooge asked.

The Ghost seemed to bow slightly, but that was its only answer. Scrooge feared this silent shape so much that his legs began to tremble. Behind that dark shroud he knew there were ghostly eyes fixed upon him.

"Ghost of the Future!" Scrooge said, "I fear you more than the other ghosts I have seen. But I know that you are here to do me good. Will you not speak to me?"

The Ghost did not reply, but pointed its hand onwards.

"Lead on!" Scrooge said. "The night is disappearing fast and I know that it is precious time for me. Lead on!"

The Ghost moved and Scrooge followed it in the shadow of his long robe, which seemed to hold him up. They entered

the city of London and came to the street where Scrooge worked. Merchants stood talking, chinking money in their pockets and looking at their watches. The Ghost pointed to a group of men and Scrooge went closer to listen to what they were saying.

"I don't know much about it," a fat man with a huge chin was saying. "I only know that he is dead."

"When did he die?" another man asked.

"Last night, I believe," the fat man replied.

"What was the matter with him?" a third man asked. "I thought he'd never die."

"God only knows," the first man said, giving an enormous yawn.

"What has he done with all his money?" a red-faced gentleman asked.

"I haven't heard yet," the man with the large chin replied. "He hasn't left it to me. That's all I know."

Everybody laughed. "It will be a cheap funeral," he went on, "because I don't know anybody who will be going to it. I suppose *we* ought to volunteer."

"I don't mind going if lunch is provided," the fat-chinned man replied, laughing.

"Whom are they talking about?" Scrooge asked.

In reply, the Ghost glided into another street where two other men were talking on the pavement.

"I know these men," Scrooge said. "They think highly of

my work. They are very rich and important. Perhaps they will have the answer."

"How are you?" the first man asked his friend. "He got what he deserved, eh?"

"So I am told," the second man replied. "It's cold, isn't it?"

"Just right for Christmas," the first man said. "Do you skate?"

Scrooge was surprised. "Why does the Ghost think this conversation is important?" he asked himself. "It has not answered my question. And where am I? Why am *I* not there?" He looked about him. "I am not standing in my usual place."

The Ghost still stood beside him, quiet and dark, its hand outstretched. Scrooge felt the Ghost's eyes staring at him.

Suddenly, he shuddered and felt *very* cold.

CHAPTER EIGHT

The Dead Man

The Ghost took Scrooge into a part of the town that he had never been before, but he recognised it from its bad reputation. The streets were dirty and narrow. The shops and houses were poor. The people were drunk and ugly. The whole place smelled of crime and dirt and misery.

Down one of these streets was a shabby shop where an old man called Joe sold bottles, old rags and anything made of metal. The floor was piled high with rusty keys, nails, chains, hinges and old iron of any sort. He huddled next to a charcoal stove made of old bricks, behind an old curtain to protect him from the cold.

Scrooge and the Ghost arrived just as a cleaning woman came into the shop carrying a bundle of clothes. A laundry woman followed her in, carrying a similar bundle. An undertaker arrived after them. They all recognised each other and burst into laughter.

"You couldn't have met in a better place," the old man said, removing the pipe from his mouth. "Now come and sit by the fire."

He raked the fire with an iron rod and put his pipe into his mouth again. While he did this, the cleaning woman threw her bundle onto the floor. Then she sat down on a stool, crossed her arms on her knees and looked at the other two.

"Don't stand there staring as if you was afraid," she said. "Who's going to find out what we've done? Who's going to miss a few things like these? Not a dead man, I suppose?"

"No, indeed," the laundry woman replied, laughing.

"If he wanted to keep his belongings after he was dead, he should have behaved better when he was alive," the cleaning woman said. "Then he would have had somebody to look after him when he was struck by Death, instead of dying there all alone."

"You never said a truer word," the other woman said. "He got what he deserved."

As they spoke, the undertaker was already opening his bag to show what he had stolen. It was not very much – a pencil-case, a pair of sleeve-buttons, a cheap brooch. Joe examined them all and wrote the price he would give with chalk on the wall.

"That's all I'll give you," he said. "I wouldn't give you another sixpence, not if you boiled me in hot water. Who's next?"

The laundry woman was next. She had brought sheets and towels, two old fashioned silver teaspoons, a pair of sugar-tongs and a few boots. Joe wrote the price on the wall.

"I always give too much to ladies," he said. "It's a weakness of mine. That's why I never make much money.

But if you ask me for another penny, I'll give you less."

"And now undo *my* bundle, Joe," the cleaning woman said.

Joe knelt down to open it. He unfastened many knots before he pulled out a heavy roll of dark material.

"Bed-curtains?" he gasped. "You don't mean that you took them down while he was lying dead on the bed?"

"Yes, I do," she replied. "Why not? And I've brought his blankets, too. And his shirt. They put it on him for the burial, but I took it off again."

Scrooge listened to this conversation in horror.

"He frightened every one of us away when he was alive," the cleaning woman laughed, "and now that he's dead, we have made money from him!"

"Spirit!" Scrooge said, shuddering from head to foot. "I understand. I understand. This dead man that they have robbed could have been me."

Scrooge suddenly cried out in terror. The scene in front of him had changed. Now he stood in front of a bed – a bare bed with no curtains around it. On this bed, beneath a ragged sheet, lay something covered up. A pale light fell upon the bed. Scrooge glanced at the Ghost. Its steady hand was pointing towards the head.

"I have only to lift that sheet to find out who the man is," Scrooge thought. "But I cannot."

CHAPTER NINE

To the Churchyard

Scrooge stood staring at the bed. "This poor creature lies in a dark and empty house," Scrooge thought, "with not a man or woman or child to remember him. I can hear rats gnawing by the fireplace. I do not dare to think what they want!"

He turned to the Ghost. "This is a dreadful place!" he cried. "I shall remember what you have taught me. Let us leave."

But still the Ghost pointed towards the head.

"I know what you are asking," Scrooge said, "but I cannot look. I cannot. Is there anybody in this town who feels any emotion because this man has died? If there is, show that person to me, I beg you!"

The Ghost spread its dark robe before him like a wing. Then he pulled it back to reveal a room where a mother sat waiting with her children. She got up from time to time and walked anxiously up and down the room. She glanced at the clock, then through the window. At last her husband returned. He was young but his face looked old and worried. But now he wore a guilty smile.

"Is it good news?" she asked him. "Will he give us time to pay the money we owe him?"

"Yes," her husband replied. "He is dead."

"Thank God!" she cried. "May God forgive me for saying so."

"I do not know who will ask us to pay back the money we owe, but we shall have saved the money by then," he said, smiling. "We may sleep well, tonight, my dear."

"But they are *pleased* that the man has died," Scrooge whispered. "Show me somebody who is upset by death of a loved one, or I shall never forget what I have just seen."

The Ghost led him to Bob Cratchit's house. The noisy little Cratchits sat as still as statues in the corner of the room. A knock came at the door and Mrs Cratchit ran to let in her husband. As he came in, each child ran to kiss him. He was cheerful at first. Then suddenly tears fell down his cheeks.

"Mr Scrooge's nephew has been very kind to me," he told them. "I have only met him once, but he noticed that I looked unhappy when he passed me in the street the other day. I told him that Tiny Tim had died. He offered to help in any way he could." Bob Cratchit looked at his family. "I am sure none of us will forget poor Tiny Tim, shall we?"

"Never, father!" they all cried, getting up to kiss him.

"Spirit," Scrooge said. "I feel that it is almost time for you to leave. Before you go, tell me the name of that man lying dead on the bed."

The Ghost of Christmas Yet to Come hurried Scrooge past his own house and past the place where he worked. The man sitting at his desk was a stranger. "Where am *I*?" Scrooge asked himself. At last, they reached an iron gate. Scrooge looked around him.

"A churchyard!" he whispered. "They have buried that wretched man, whose name I still do not know."

The Ghost stood among the graves and pointed down to one of them. Scrooge walked towards it, trembling.

"Before I reach that grave, answer me one question," Scrooge said. "Are these things the shadows of the things that will be, or are they shadows of things that might be?"

"The future can be changed if the person chooses to change," the Ghost replied, pointing to the grave.

Scrooge crept towards it, shuddering. He read the name that the Ghost traced with his finger on the headstone: EBENEZER SCROOGE. Scrooge sank to his knees.

"I was that man laying on the bed!" he cried. "No, Spirit! Oh no, no!" Scrooge clutched its robe. "Listen to me. I am not the man I was. I have changed. Please tell me that I may change the shadows of my past by changing my behaviour?"

He saw the Ghost's hand tremble.

"I will celebrate Christmas with all my heart," Scrooge said. "And I will be kind all through the year. The Spirits of all Three Ghosts will remind me. I shall never forget the lessons they have taught me. Oh tell me that my name will not be written on this gravestone!"

In his agony, Scrooge knelt and caught hold of the

Ghost's hand, but the Ghost pushed him away.

"I beg you, tell me!" Scrooge cried.

But the Ghost was stronger than Scrooge. He pushed him away again. And Scrooge held up his hands to beg one last time.

CHAPTER TEN

The End of It

As Scrooge begged, the Ghost's robe and hood began to shrink and change into the shape of a bedpost.

"I'm in my own bed!" Scrooge cried. "I'm in my own room! I'm still alive and I have time to put everything right. Oh, Jacob Marley! I thank Christmas for changing me!" Scrooge's face was wet with tears. "My bed-curtains are still here," he said. "I am still here. I can chase away the shadows of those terrible things that might happen. I *know* I can!"

Scrooge got dressed as he spoke to himself. "I don't know what to do!" he said, laughing and crying at the same time. "I am as light as a feather. I am as happy as an angel. I am as merry as a schoolboy. A Merry Christmas to everybody. A Happy New Year to all the world."

He glanced around his room. "There's the door by which the Ghost of Jacob Marley entered," he said. "There's the room where the Ghost of Christmas Present sat. There's the window where I saw the other ghosts. It's all true! It *did* happen!"

Scrooge started to laugh. And for a man who hadn't laughed for years, it was a splendid laugh and the first of many laughs to come. The church bells began to ring out.

Scrooge ran to the window and put out his head. No fog, no mist. The night was clear, bright and cold. The air was fresh and sweet.

"What day is it?" Scrooge called down to a boy dressed in his best clothes.

"Eh?" the boy said in surprise. "It's Christmas day, of course!"

"It's Christmas day," Scrooge whispered to himself. "I haven't missed it. The Ghosts *have* done all their work in one night." He leaned further out of the window. "Now, my fine fellow, do you know the meat shop in the next street but one, at the corner?" he shouted. "Go and buy that big turkey for me and have it sent to this address. I'll give you a shilling." He rubbed his hands together happily. "Bob Cratchit won't know who sent it. It's twice the size of Tiny Tim."

Scrooge laughed as he paid for the turkey. He laughed as he paid the boy. He laughed as he looked at the doorknocker. And he laughed even more loudly when he sat down again in his chair and laughed until he cried. Then he dressed in his best clothes and went down into the street.

By this time, people were walking out as he had seen them with the Ghost of Christmas Present. Walking with his hands behind his back, Scrooge smiled at everybody. He looked so happy that three or four gentlemen said, "Good morning, sir, a Merry Christmas to you!"

"That is the happiest sound I have ever heard," Scrooge

said to himself.

He had not gone far when he met one of the gentlemen who had come to his office collecting money for the poor. Scrooge shook his hand. "How do you do?" he said. "A Merry Christmas to you, sir."

"Mr Scrooge?" the gentleman asked.

"Yes," Scrooge replied. "That is my name and I am afraid you may not wish to hear it. May I ask you to forgive me? And I should like you to accept..." Scrooge whispered the amount in his ear.

"Lord bless me!" the gentleman said. "My dear Scrooge, are you serious?"

"Please accept it," Scrooge replied, "it will make up for all the years I have refused to give money to the poor."

The gentleman shook his hand and Scrooge walked on. He never dreamt that any walk could give him so much pleasure. In the afternoon, he made his way towards his nephew's house. He passed the door a dozen times before he found the courage to knock on it. The servant showed Scrooge upstairs to the dining room, but he did not go in straight away. He peeped around the door.

"Fred!" Scrooge called out at last.

"Why, bless my soul!" Fred cried. "Who is that?"

"Your Uncle Scrooge," he replied. "I have come to eat Christmas dinner with you. Will you let me in, Fred?"

Fred almost shook Scrooge's arm off. He felt at home in five minutes. It was a wonderful party, with wonderful games and wonderful happiness.

Scrooge was early in his office the next morning. He wanted to be first, to catch Bob Cratchit coming in late. The clock struck nine. No Bob. A quarter past nine. No Bob.

He came in eighteen and a half minutes late. He took off

his hat as he opened the door, sat on his stool and began to write.

"Good morning," Scrooge growled, trying to make his voice as unpleasant as it used to be. "What do you mean, starting work at this time of the day?"

"I am very sorry, sir," Bob replied.

"Step this way, sir, if you please," Scrooge said.

"It's only once a year, sir," Bob begged, trembling. "I shall not do it again."

"A Merry Christmas, Bob," Scrooge said suddenly, slapping him on the back. "I shall raise your salary and try to help your family. We shall discuss it this afternoon, Bob. Now make up the fire."

At first, Bob Cratchit thought that Scrooge had gone mad! But Scrooge did even more than he had promised that day. He became like a second father to Tiny Tim, who did *not* die He became a good friend to everybody everywhere. Some people laughed at the change in him, but he let them laugh. He was happy and that was quite enough for him. Ebenezer Scrooge never saw a ghost again. And people always said that he knew how to celebrate Christmas better than anybody.

Let that be true of us all.